Mad at Mommy

KOMAKO SAKAI

ARTHUR A. LEVINE BOOKS

An Imprint of Scholastic Inc.

Mommy, I — I —

I AM SO MAD AT YOU!

You always sleep late,
especially on Saturdays.
Always and always.

You always watch your shows

and never let me
watch cartoons.

You yell for no reason.

And you always tell
me to hurry up —

hurry up —

hurry up —

but then you never
hurry up yourself.

And —
And you're always late picking me up from school.
Then you forget to wash all my clothes.
See! I'm wearing the same socks as yesterday!
And —

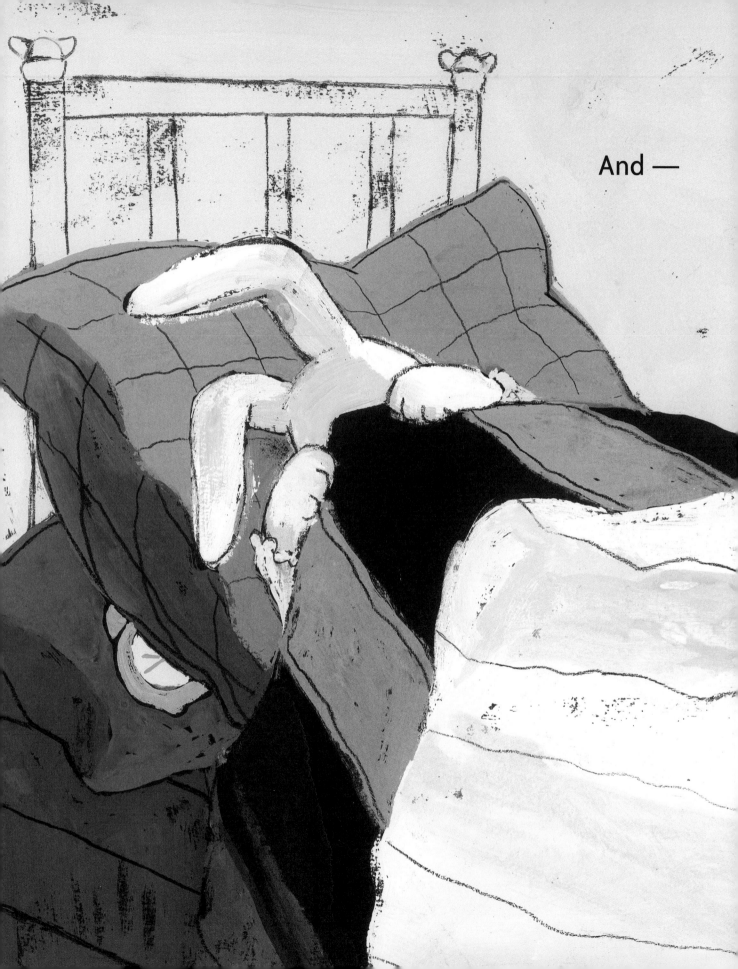

And —

And —

And —

And —

And you say you can't marry me,

not even when I get bigger.

But I'm gonna get bigger
and **bigger**
and **bigger**

and I'll do whatever I want!

So I'm really mad at you, Mommy.
So mad I'm gonna LEAVE.
I'm going someplace far, far away.

GOOD-BYE.

"Mommy?"

"Sweetie?
Did you forget something?"

"Yeah, I forgot my . . . ball.
I need it."

"Mommy?"

"Yes?"

"Did you miss me?"

"SO much!"

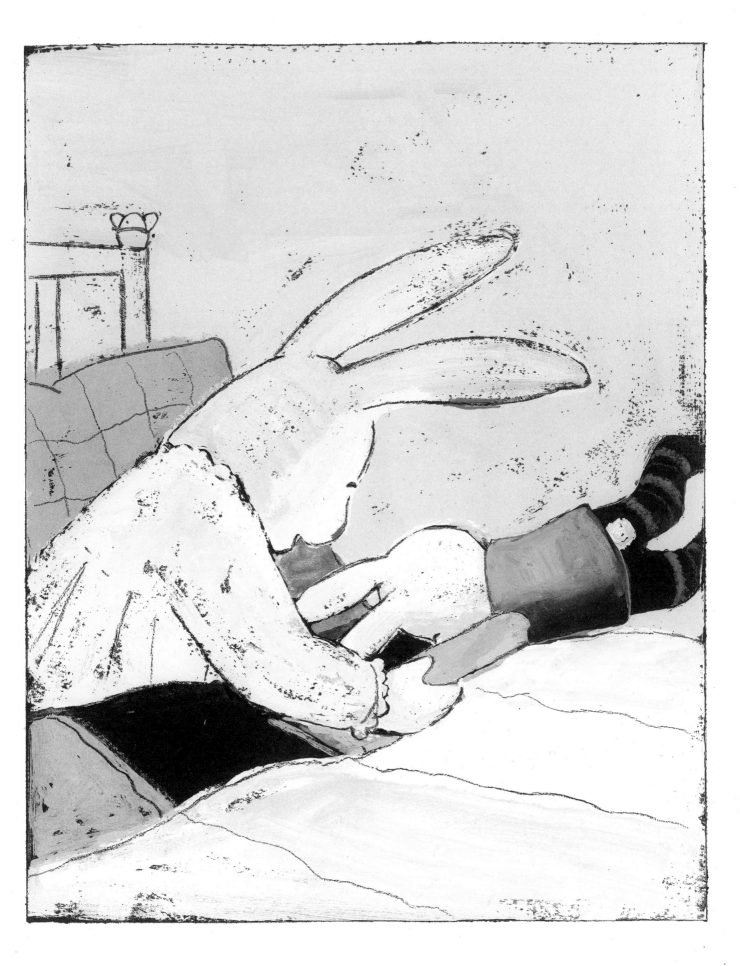

Text and illustrations copyright © 2000 by Komako Sakai · First published in Japan in 2000 by Bunkeido Ltd., under the title *Boku Okâsan no Koto.* · All rights reserved. Published by Arthur A. Levine Books, an imprint of Scholastic Inc., *Publishers since 1920*, by arrangement with Bunkeido Ltd., through the Japanese Foreign Rights Centre. SCHOLASTIC and the LANTERN LOGO are trademarks and/or registered trademarks of Scholastic Inc. · No part of this publication may be reproduced, stored in a retrieval system, or transmitted in any form or by any means, electronic, mechanical, photocopying, recording, or otherwise, without written permission of the publisher. For information regarding permission, write to Scholastic Inc., Attention: Permissions Department, 557 Broadway, New York, NY 10012. · Library of Congress Cataloging-in-Publication Data · Sakai, Komako, 1966- · [Boku okasan no koto. English] · Mad at Mommy / by Komako Sakai. — 1st American ed. p. cm. · Summary: A little rabbit is very angry at his mother, and he tells her the reasons why. · ISBN 978-0-545-21209-0 (alk. paper) · [1. Mother and child—Fiction. 2. Anger—Fiction. 3. Rabbits—Fiction.] I. Title. PZ7.S143943Mad 2010 · [E]—dc22 · 2009042295 · Design by Lillie Howard · 10 9 8 7 6 5 4 3 2 1 10 11 12 13 14 · Printed in Singapore 46 · First American edition, October 2010